The Sneaky Skeleton

Halloween Madness - Book 5
A Starlight Investigation Short Story

Marnie Atwell

The Halloween Madness Series is written by an Australian author who uses Australian spelling. This book contains 21,400 words.

ISBN: 978-0-6450281-9-5

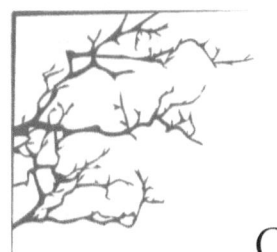

Chapter One

It was official; the woman standing quietly behind the counter was bonkers. Callum glared at her with rising levels of frustration. She merely smiled at him. Her face radiated a classic kind of beauty designed to disarm her opponent into missing the signs of craziness that lay beneath her gentle eyes.

He glanced at her name badge, his scowl deepening further. Marguerite. A name that reflected her exotic beauty perfectly. He would not allow himself to be swayed by her appearance or the sultry tones of her voice. She *would* give in to his wishes. They all did in the end.

"Now then, Marguerite. Please listen to me carefully. My name is Liam Force, and I am here to pick up a four-door sedan. Like I said on the phone, I don't care what make or model the car is, as long as it is not black."

"I am sorry, Mr Force, but I cannot provide that for you. You have reserved and paid for one of our mid-sized removal trucks. As requested, there are motorcycle straps located in the cargo bed. One of our mechanics fitted tie-down points as instructed."

"I did not ask for that," Callum said gruffly, finding it difficult to keep his voice calm.

The change in his tone forced her eyes to blink rapidly in response. Still, she gathered herself swiftly and displayed no other sign that his deteriorating mood had affected her in any way.

"Would you like to listen to the recording?"

"I beg your pardon?" He splayed his fingers across the counter's surface.

She lowered her eyes to appraise the risk level to herself. Once she was satisfied they were not going to curl into fists, she repeated her statement. "We record all of our bookings. Would you care to listen to the audio file?"

"Sure," he said with a wicked grin.

The widening of her eyes was barely perceptible. Yet Callum, being a super-human, had no trouble noticing the slight movement. He squinted his eyes marginally as he studied her reaction. He was beginning to think she was becoming frightened that he would hurt her. The other micro-movements he detected in her facial expression, and the enhanced allure of her natural scent indicated that she found his menacing grin attractive. Perhaps he could use that to his advantage.

Marguerite strode from the counter quickly and spoke to someone out of view. Within seconds, a burly guy with a bushy moustache and long beard appeared in the doorway. He wore a white singlet that showed off his impressive muscles and tribal tattoos and a pair of jeans covered in grease and oil. Steel-capped boots covered his feet, and the top of his head was completely bald.

"Mr Force, great to see you again," he said in a gravelly tone. From the smell of his breath, Callum deduced his larynx's hoarseness was an unfortunate side effect of his nicotine habit.

"Is it?" Callum queried, wondering how many times Liam had required the use of a rental vehicle.

"Sure," he grinned. "We love to see your face around here." Lowering his voice to a whisper, he said, "Though, there hasn't been another incident that requires your attention."

"Glad to hear it, Butch," Callum nodded, saying the name stitched in block letters on the upper right-hand side of the chest area. "If we could clear up this little misunderstanding, I would really like to be on my way. Friends are expecting me."

"Yeah, it's not a good idea to keep them waiting. A lot of bad things can happen on country roads. It's not such a big deal in the city where there are loads of people milling about, but out here on the country roads without another soul for miles. Well, in some instances . . ."

"Exactly," Callum stated solemnly, leaning on his elbows and clasping his hands together. "Let's hear the audio, then."

The bell dinged above the door, interrupting their conversation. Butch's eyes flicked to the newcomer, reflecting their surprise. Callum glanced over his shoulder, then swiftly straightened his spine. Displaying some confusion of his own, he walked towards the newcomer and brought his arms up. He gripped the guy by his upper arms and said, "Brother."

Force returned Callum's grip, peering into eyes identical to his own, and said, "How the hell are you, Liam?"

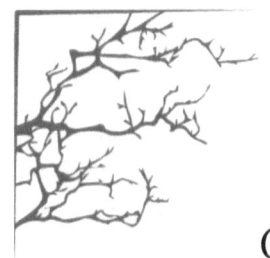

Chapter Two

The boys released one another and returned to the counter. Liam's grin was genuine, while Callum's was entirely forced. Liam held his hands out for the keys to the truck while Callum simply looked on. He realised that Liam had changed their plans and couldn't wait to get outside to find out what was going on.

Butch turned his attention to Callum with a questioning look. Callum merely nodded, consenting silently to taking delivery of whatever vehicle Liam had specified. With a shrug of his shoulders, Butch retrieved the keys from below the counter and called for Marguerite's return. He held them in front of Callum and said, "You'll need to sign the paperwork before you leave."

She did a double-take as she approached the counter but, as before, quickly gathered herself together. Butch handed her the keys and asked, "You right here, love?"

She nodded her head, "Yep."

He turned to Callum before taking his leave, "I'd like to talk about this sometime." Butch pointed his finger at Liam and then swung it back around to Callum.

Callum shrugged, "What's to tell? I have a twin brother. He's helping me move."

Butch made an inexplicable sound before returning to his previous duties. Marguerite pulled out the paperwork and handed it to Callum. She studied them both as he filled in the boxes and signed where indicated. She requested to see his driver's licence, and Callum was pleased that Liam had had the foresight to mail it to him in advance. He pulled it from his pocket and handed it to her. She checked the signature and said, "Your likeness to one another is uncanny. I've never seen twins so close in appearance."

"You've seen a lot of twins?" Liam asked sceptically,

"Yep. It has always been an interest of mine. I wrote a research paper on the genes of identical siblings while studying for my doctorate. I studied hundreds of twins while completing my research. There are *always* slight variances that a discerning eye can spot. Yet, I can't see any of those with the pair of you. Fascinating."

"Maybe you just need to spend more time with us," Callum suggested helpfully, leaning forward to rest his arms on the counter.

Marguerite reflected his move and studied him more closely.

"Not today!" Force said a little louder than intended. "We have to get going, Liam. People are waiting anxiously for the arrival of the truck."

Callum stood up with reluctance. "You are right. Maybe we can come back when we are done."

"Speak for yourself," Force growled. "I haven't seen my wife in over two weeks. I think I will be a little busy."

Callum widened his eyes. The change in Force's demeanour was staggering. Liam was usually way more laid back than him. Callum brimmed with curiosity. He looked at Marguerite with some regret, "Some other time, then."

"Sure," she replied, still puzzling over their lack of uniqueness. She pushed the keys towards Callum and said, "See you in a week?"

"Yes," he winked, scooping up the keyring and then heading for the door.

Force turned on his heel and followed, refusing to glance back at the woman. He knew she would be wracking her brain for a plausible solution that didn't exist to human knowledge. Callum reached the door before he realised he had left his bag on the floor in front of the counter. He hurried back with a goofy grin on his face. He leant forward to reach the straps, jiggling the backpack so that it didn't flip over his head. He stood up and asked, "Why are you working here if you are studying for your doctorate?"

"This is my uncle's shop. I help him out whenever I can."

"Right," Callum said, with a curiousness to his tone.

Marguerite declined to explain the vast differences in their appearances or clarify the specificities of her studies. She raised an eyebrow, and Callum decided it was time to follow Liam out of the building before he blew his chances of successfully asking her out on a date.

The men stepped out into the sunshine and felt their skin tighten instantly with the heat. Callum fanned himself with his hand, which had no impact at all. "How can you live here?" he asked. "It's so humid."

Force shrugged his shoulders, "You get used to it. Better than being cold."

"You think?" Callum asked, preferring to be rugged up in winter clothes and snuggling under heavy blankets at night.

"We'll go for a swim later. You'll love it."

"You have a pool?" Callum grinned.

"Not yet," Force admitted, "but we have a lovely creek that runs through the property. It is deep enough in some places to swim."

"Nice," he replied, attempting to hand over the keys.

Liam held up his hands. "You are driving."

Callum frowned. "I don't know where to go. It would make more sense for you to drive."

"It would, but my plans have changed. Open up the back, will you?"

Callum did as requested and found a ramp sitting on the tray inside. He slid it out and peered at it intently. Then he scoured the plate and put two and two together.

He hooked the ramp to the ridge that had been welded in and heard the rumble of Force's bike starting up. Moving out of the way, he watched Force expertly load the bike onto the truck and then climbed inside to help him secure it. Callum placed his bags beside the bike and then jumped down and headed for the cab. He looked over his shoulder. "Are you coming?"

"Yeah, be there in a minute," Force responded, taking a small box from his pocket and placing it in a side pocket of the backpack. He exited the truck and locked the back doors, then climbed into the passenger seat. "You do know how to drive one of these, Callum?"

"Sure," he grinned, putting one foot on the brake and pushing in the clutch with the other while he turned the key. He left the parking lot without any issues and quickly settled in on the highway. "So, where are we going?" With Callum's permission, Force tapped into his mind and provided him with directions. "Why am I driving?"

"I want you to pretend to be me for a little bit longer."

"How long?" Callum queried.

"Your entire stay." Liam's response was resolute.

"What? Why?"

"I want to play Wade." Liam regarded the scenery outside the passenger window, afraid of what he would see on Callum's face.

"You want to pretend you are married to April? Won't that be a little awkward, seeing as though your cases sometimes overlap?"

"I love her, Callum, and I think she has feelings for me. She just won't admit it. I need to know if I have a chance with her."

"Relationships between Gatherers are forbidden."

"If that were the case, Rochelle and Toren would have been punished years ago."

"They have been. Toren is now a vampire. You don't think the royals had a hand in that?"

"Of course not. Rochelle and Toren were together five hundred years, Callum. The royals would not have let them go on for so long if they were going to uphold an outdated law."

"Time works differently on Mystique. Five centuries here is a blink of an eye there, or have you forgotten so quickly?"

Liam hated to admit that he had, so he kept quiet. Was it possible that the Queen had something to do with Toren's "accident"? April had thought so at the time, but he hadn't wanted to consider the possibility that she was right. Was a relationship with April worth the risk that something might happen to them also? He thought so. They would just have to be more careful. Everyone knew about Rochelle and Toren, including the chroniclers at Starlight Investigations. Perhaps if the relationship remained a secret among April, Callum, Scout, Briella, and himself, they could avoid the penalties of their forbidden love.

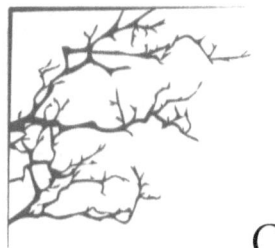

Chapter Three

Force consulted his watch as they neared the welcome sign to Glenvale. Settlement of the property was still an hour away, so he suggested to Callum that they make their way to the pub for a nice cold beer and the pub special.

There was plenty of room in the carpark for the truck, and it would give Force an opportunity to test April's reaction to his husbandly displays of affection with minimal witnesses. They removed the motorbike safely, retrieved Callum's bags from the cargo area, and then made their way inside the pub. April was rounding the bar when she spotted their arrival. She stopped in her tracks to stare at them, because they were not dressed as she was expecting them to be.

Callum was wearing Force's trademark outfit: full-length pants, lace-up shoes and a singlet top, all in black. Liam dressed how he imagined Wade would appear in casual circumstances. A pale blue button-up shirt partnered with knee-length cargo pants in cream and brown pull-on shoes with no socks. Although April was certain the guys had switched places, she decided to play along with their little charade to see where it would lead rather than call them out on it.

Liam stepped forward to greet her, a broad grin on his face. "Hey there, beautiful," he said, wrapping his arms around her waist and giving her a short but profoundly expressive kiss. He lifted his chin and rested it gently on the top of her head, hugging her close. "I've missed you."

April's thoughts ran wild. That kiss had been far more emotional than she had expected to receive and affected her body in ways she hadn't anticipated. She noticed the smiles on the faces of the patrons, who had turned in their chairs to observe their greeting. Momentarily lost for words, she returned the sentiment, "I've missed you, too." She wrapped her arms around his waist and glanced at her shoulder, confirming that goosebumps had risen on her skin the moment his lips had touched her own. A tell-tale sign of the tingling sensation she had just experienced Also confirming in her mind that the boys had switched places.

She lifted her hands slightly and brushed the bottom of his backpack. 'You packed light," she said, pulling back to see the straps wrapped around his shoulders.

He tapped the bag by his side with his foot, "There's another bag here." He took a deep breath and began pulling the bag off his shoulders. As he slid the zipper open on a side pocket, he said, "I got you something. I hope you like it."

April looked at the expertly gift-wrapped box with her stomach in her throat. It was the perfect size for housing a ring. She slowly raised her eyes to his. She hoped he noticed her apprehension and silent plea that he did not embarrass her in front of the townspeople. "Go on, love. Open it," he encouraged with a gentle smile.

She took the gift with trembling fingers and untied the silver bow. Then, she instigated a delaying tactic by searching the wrapping paper for the beginning of the sticky tape, while her brain went into overdrive. She glanced down at the set of rings resting on her ring finger, which she had bought earlier as props for their fake marriage, desperately trying to remember if she had informed Liam of her purchase. The fact that she had feelings for Liam which she was desperately trying to quash was playing havoc with her brain. Because, if her feelings were reciprocated, then they were in a whole world of trouble. Force chuckled good naturedly, "Just rip it open, love. You won't be needing the paper."

April winced as the patrons at the bar began to chuckle themselves, then covered their faux pas with fake coughs. *"Rip it off like a band-aid,"* she thought. *"You are supposed to believe that Callum is the one giving you the gift."* In no time, the box was glaring at her, daring her to open it. She breathed in slowly and opened the lid to find a silver heart-shaped pendant with a sapphire in the middle. "Oh," she sighed. "It's beautiful."

Force grinned from ear to ear as he removed the pendant from its gift box and released the clasp. He moved to stand behind her, then placed it gently against her skin. He refastened the chain and lightly kissed the nape of her neck before fixing her ponytail in place.

"Why don't I put your stuff upstairs while you claim us a table," Callum suggested, experiencing the first rumblings of hunger.

"Great idea," April said, lightly fingering the pendant.

Force took her by the arm and led her to the dining area. Callum raced upstairs with bags in hand and realised he didn't know which room was theirs. He briefly considered tapping into Liam's mind but figured he could find it on his own. Callum would easily spot April and Liam's signatures on the doors that led to their rooms.

He entered Liam's room without any trouble and set the bags on the floor. He used the facilities and was exiting the bathroom when the fairies burst into the room. Scout and Briella hesitated slightly as their eyes fell on him. He was so close to Liam's appearance that they had to blink to make sure they were interpreting the impersonator in front of them properly. Briella seeing an opportunity blooming before her muttered to Scout, "Follow my lead." They fluttered swiftly towards him, shouting words while projecting their thoughts to ensure Callum heard them. *"Quickly, Force, Stubs is at it again!"* screamed Briella.

Scout shouted, *"Stubs has got himself into trouble again!"*

Callum raised his hands and took a step backwards, "Whoa there, ladies. You've got the wrong man."

Scout and Briella glared at him. "How can you say that?" Briella cringed, flapping her wings furiously as she hovered in front of him. "I thought you liked Stubs."

"I am sure *Liam* does," Callum assured her. "My name is Callum. Sorry, but I have no idea what you are talking about."

Scout eyed him critically. "I realise that Gatherers have an amazing ability to replicate any living creature of their choosing. I am also aware, as incredible as you all are, that none of you can replicate a person they are copying perfectly. There is always a difference that allows those in the know to identify the impersonator as an imposter. I don't know what game you are playing, Force, but Stubs is in a lot of trouble. If you don't help him right now, he might severely injure himself."

Callum considered transforming back into his own body but was worried he would forget to change again before heading downstairs. He deemed it would be quicker to allow the fairies to lead him to the issue and attempt to fix the situation than to explain his current circumstances.

"We'd better hurry then," he stated calmly, waiting for them to show him the way. They flew towards the window and exited through the slight opening. He dashed around the coffee table and threw the window open, managing to spot Briella's feet disappearing through the window further down the building. Callum stood indecisively for a few seconds, wondering whether to follow the route the fairies had taken or to use the usual method for entering and exiting a room.

He chose the latter, closing the window until it was back to its original position and exiting through the front door. Callum was inside April's room in moments. He found himself the centre of attention to four kittens exuding boundless amounts of energy. The mother cat merely gave him a cursory glance before resuming the action of washing her face.

"Over here," the fairies called to him.

Callum closed the door behind him and stepped carefully around the kittens who were attempting to use his shoelaces as playthings.

The fairies lingered over a coffee table that had an object covered by a tablecloth on top. "So, what is the problem?" Callum frowned.

"Stubs is in there, and he can't find his way out," Scout howled.

"Stubs is stuck in my house," Briella shrieked.

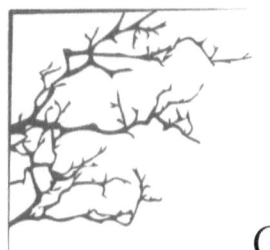

Chapter Four

Callum bent down, grabbed a corner of the tablecloth, and pulled it away with a flourish. He squatted on his haunches and peered through the windows of Briella's new home-away-from-home. He marvelled at the quality that had gone into building this amazing piece of art.

"This is awesome," Callum uttered, stating the obvious.

"It sure is," Briella replied with excitement. "I knew it was going to be amazing, but I had no idea it would be as wonderful as this."

They were looking at a two-storey Victorian-style house with a grey slated roof and their very own turret, large bay windows and a cute little porch. The walls were an off-white colour, and leadlight decorated the windows. The curtains were white with red trim. Four stairs led to the landing, which matched the roof paint, and white rail posts bordered the front porch. It was far larger than Scout had expected but also the cutest house she had ever seen. Off to the right was a garage which housed their remote-controlled jeep and a new motorcycle with one helmet hanging from the handlebar and another resting on the seat.

Scout cast a critical eye over their new abode. "Are you sure you haven't seen this before?"

Briella could barely draw her eyes away to reply, "No. Why do you ask?"

Scout flew in for a closer inspection, "It looks very similar to the house of horrors you drew the other day. Only, the windows are intact, and the paintwork is beautiful, and there is no chamber of terror on the first floor."

Briella peered in through the windows. "Look at the furniture. April has spared no expense."

Scout sucked in a breath, "Take a look at your kitchen, Briella."

Briella fluttered over to Scout and, rather than appreciating the gorgeous cabinetry, her eyes rested on the new appliances sitting on the bench. Her hands flew to her chest as she said, "Oh my goodness, Scout. Look at that coffee machine. I'll be able to make my own cappuccinos and it matches in colour and style with the toaster and kettle. It's absolutely perfect."

Scout's excitement dipped considerably as she realised she may never get Briella to return to the fairy way of life. Especially considering they may not have as much time together as she had hoped due to their locating responsibilities. Unless she could convince April that Briella would be better off returning to her natural state, Briella would become an outcast amongst the fairies when the purge arrives. Scout shuddered to think of Briella drinking coffee and eating toast.

Callum observed them with a confused frown. "I thought we were rescuing Stubs from whatever predicament he had gotten himself into."

Scout waved her hand in the air. "That was just an excuse to induce you to give us a look at Briella's new home. April wouldn't allow us to see it."

Callum rose to his feet. "You used me. You knew I was Callum all along."

Scout and Briella glanced over their shoulders. "Yep."

"Thanks for that," Briella replied sweetly.

"Rude," Callum strode towards the front door.

Briella flew after him, *"Where are you going?"*

"Downstairs for lunch. Liam and April are waiting for me."

"Why are they waiting for you? Why didn't you stay downstairs with them?"

"They were getting us a table for lunch and I wanted to bring my bags upstairs to get them out of the way."

He opened the door. "You can't leave the tablecloth off the house. April will kill us."

"You should have thought of that before," he scowled.

"You let the kittens out," Briella smirked. "April is going to be really mad when I tell her what you did."

"So, you are planning on blackmailing me into keeping your little ploy a secret. Is that it?" he asked, scooping the kittens up and returning them to the room.

"I suppose so," Briella shrugged her shoulders.

"Fine, but you owe me a favour."

"No, I don't. I won't tell April you allowed the kittens to escape if you don't tell her Scout and I have seen our new house. One good deed paid in full by the other."

"Except your little secret is worth a lot more than my little secret, don't you think?"

"No," Briella stamped her foot mid-air.

"Let it go," Scout advised Briella. "We will owe you a favour. Now, will you please put the cover back on before April or Force come up to see what is taking you so long?"

"I don't think that is going to be an issue," Callum muttered, actioning their request. "Is there anything else?"

"How long will you be staying?" Briella asked tersely.

Callum debated not answering her but chose to rise above her level, "A week, most likely."

"I see," Briella scowled, worrying over the favour he might ask of her in the future.

Scout frowned, thinking about their Gatherers' travelling accessories. "That is a lot of luggage you brought with you for a week. Surely, you would only need a couple of changes of clothes."

"Not all of it is for me." He walked towards the door.

"Who else is it for?" Scout queried.

He eyed her carefully and realised her curiosity was genuine. "I brought a house warming present for April and Liam," he admitted.

"What is it?" she fluttered closer.

"Something that will fit in perfectly with the theme of the party."

"Like what?" Briella asked, her interest piqued.

"Never you mind," he answered, pointing his finger at them both. "All will be revealed in good time. Now, don't you go snooping!"

"How are we supposed to do that? We couldn't even get a tablecloth off the house. How are we supposed to get your bag open?"

"How indeed?" he answered with a raised eyebrow. Callum stepped outside, confirming none of the kittens had followed him. He then made his way downstairs, wondering if the fairies would leave his stuff alone or if he had just provided them with their next irresistible quest for discovery.

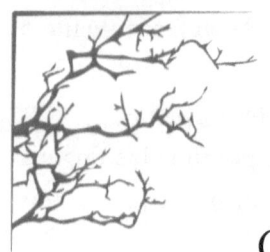

Chapter Five

Briella turned to Scout, who was already viewing her with a rising eagerness for a new adventure. The opportunity to take a tour through Briella's new house had disappeared. They would have to be content with the images they had attained of the outside and what they had been able to observe through the windows. The fairies would only have to wait a few more days before the building was placed in their new fairy garden, and they were able to take a look inside.

"What do you think?" Briella asked with an innocence that belied her words.

"I think we should take a look at what's inside Callum's bag."

Briella nodded her head, "My thoughts exactly. Goodness knows we don't need any more surprises before the townsfolk descend on us. Forewarned is forearmed, don't they say?"

Scout frowned, "Who's they?"

"They. Them." Briella replied, waving her hand in the air. "You know, those people."

Scout had no idea but quickly shrugged it off. She fluttered towards the window with Briella in hot pursuit. They entered Force's window and landed beside the two bags lying neatly on the floor. They looked at all of the zippers on the backpack and decided to start with the other first. It was a sports bag that had only one compartment and a zipper that ran across the middle from one end to the other.

They wrapped their hands around the eye of the zipper and flapped their wings furiously, barely making any headway. The going was tough; the bag appeared to be reasonably new. Scout let the zipper go with a huff. "Why don't we try flying in a forward direction? It might be easier going."

Briella considered the idea. "It's worth a try."

They turned themselves around and took up their positions, then flapped their wings like crazy. The pull tab flipped over, taking the fairies with it. It all happened so fast that they forgot to let go and found themselves lying face-up on the scratchy material. Scout rolled onto her side, bringing Briella's shocked face into view. "Perhaps we should see if we can find a lever of sorts to hook into the pull tab and use that to help us get the darned thing open."

Briella raised herself slightly, using her elbows as support. "Why don't you just use your magic to get it to open?"

"For the same reason, I didn't use it on the tablecloth. I am placing my magic on hold unless there is an absolute emergency, until Halloween is over and your magic returns to normal."

"Then I guess we won't know what is in the bag."

Scout flew to the small opening they had created. She stretched out her arms and positioned her fingers so they formed the shape of a square. Scout then measured the gap to see if her hands would fit. She rose into the air excitedly and flew to the cupboard that housed their lanterns. "A little bit of magic dust in this situation won't hurt anybody's feelings," she said, justifying her newest idea.

Briella merely rolled her eyes. "We aren't climbing in there without knowing what is in there. It could be dangerous."

"It could also be something like a costume that Callum is planning on wearing to the party."

"Why would Callum bring a costume as a house-warming gift?" Briella queried.

"Why not?" Scout replied, grasping the lantern's handle and preparing her body for the expulsion of her fairy magic.

"Can we try something else before you do that?" Briella asked.

Scout glanced up and saw the look on her friend's face. "Sure," she said gently. "What do you have in mind?"

"I was thinking that if we grabbed the pull tab firmly and held it at the angle of a pram's handle, we might have more luck in getting it to shift."

"That's a great idea," Scout said, placing the lantern gently on the kitchen counter. "Let's give it a go."

They took up their positions and held the zipper as Briella suggested. They were able to get the zip to open the entire distance. The girls high-fived each other and began the arduous task of pulling the material aside to see what lay inside.

They didn't have to pull it too far before Briella began shrieking. Scout got such a fright she let go of the material which was too heavy for Briella to hold in position by herself. She went flying inside the bag as the fabric returned to its former position. When Briella realised the horror of her situation, the screaming intensified. As happens when Briella becomes frightened, her body releases an abundance of fairy dust over the very thing that terrifies her.

"Get me out of here, Scout, before it rises and hurts me."

Scout was tugging against the fabric as hard as she could. "What is it?" she screamed.

"You don't want to know," Briella cried, sobs of terror causing her nose to run. She sniffed a few times as she attempted to breach the surface. Every time she moved a leg, she slid further inside the bag. There was not enough room in there for her to spread her wings and fly, and the surface she stood on was too slippery to get a good grip and climb her way out. "I'm going to die," Briella moaned.

"No, you are not," Scout scowled, heaving as hard as she could. The bag swallowed its second victim for the day. "Briella," Scout cried out as she toppled forward. She felt every thump her body made against the smooth, vertical substances until she landed on a horizontal beam. "Oomph," she huffed as the air left her body in a gush.

"Are you all right?" Briella queried.

"I think so," Scout stated, carefully raising herself onto hands and knees. "Where are you?" she asked, then wobbled as the structure beneath her began to move. "What is happening?"

"I believe the remnants of this body are coming to life," Briella informed her. "I might have gotten some fairy dust on it."

"Remnants of a body?" Scout gurgled.

"I believe that Callum has brought us some human remains for our Halloween party."

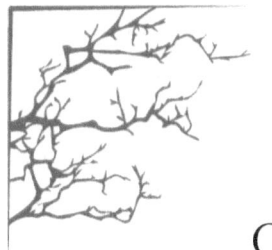

Chapter Six

Scout couldn't wait to get out of there and away from the bones. She couldn't for the life of her work out how she was going to accomplish such a feat. Her arms swung wide as the ground beneath her fell away. Her fingers searched frantically for something small enough to wrap around and rough enough to be able to get a firm hold.

Desperation driving her, Scout had gone into survival mode. She was not conscious of what was happening around her, not to mention that she was totally in the dark. So, she was surprised to find herself suddenly outside the bag and tumbling through the air. Her wings managed to stabilise her. Scout raised her hands to her head, which was feeling quite dizzy by now.

When her brain stopped spinning, she looked around and spotted Briella a few metres away. She also held her head and appeared a few shades paler. Scout flew towards her, choosing to take the longer route, avoiding the bag entirely, afraid of what might jump out of the opening. "What just happened?"

"I don't know," Briella replied shakily. "I'm glad we are out, though," she peered at the bag fearfully. "Maybe we should close the zipper."

Scout shook her head, "I'm not going anywhere near that thing. Are you sure there are bones in there?"

"Yep, I saw them myself before I fell inside. Why would Callum bring us bones?"

"I don't know. I don't know anything about him."

"Maybe we should steer clear of him."

"Agreed," Scout said with enthusiasm. "Why don't we get out of here?"

Briella frowned, "He will know we have looked inside his bag."

"So what? What is he going to do about it?"

"I think I got some magic on them," Briella mentioned softly.

"We can sit on the windowsill for a little while to see if anything happens if you like."

"I think that would be for the best," Briella agreed. "What do we do if they come out of the bag and start hitting us like that pencil did when I was drawing that time?"

"We will wrangle them inside the cage just like we did with the pencil."

"Cool," Briella nodded, taking a seat in the sunshine while Scout flew next door to retrieve the cage, just in case. The fairies weren't aware there was a full-sized skeleton in the bag. As far as they knew, there was just a bunch of bones in the bag. While the cage would be big enough to fit a hand, it would definitely not fit a skeleton in there. For now, however, Scout had managed to calm Briella's nerves and prevented more magic dust from being expelled.

They sat that way for quite a while. There was no indication that the contents of the bag were going to come to life. They talked about moving to the new house, which reminded Scout to ask Force to collect her tree-house from the Hinterlands.

They wondered how the Gatherers would explain the magnitude of props that would be available for the townspeople to enjoy at the party in the limited time they had available. Not to mention the two-storey house that would suddenly appear on their newly acquired property with creatures inside that would scare the pants off the most tranquil person in the world.

Briella, who was not one to sit still for any length of time, soon became bored. "I think that I was mistaken. Perhaps it is safe to close the zip and head back to the kittens. They will be out in the yard soon, and it won't be as much fun to be around them."

"Why is that?" Scout asked, thinking they were the perfect incentive to pull Briella away from her television shows and return her to a more natural state.

"There won't be anything for them to investigate or crawl over in the yard."

"You would be surprised," Scout said. "I'll put this back where it belongs and give you a hand." She scrambled to her feet, grabbed the handle of the cage, and then returned to the room next door.

Briella flew over to the bag and grabbed hold of the pull tab in an attempt to close the bag herself. She placed it in the pram-handle position and dashed forward. The zip didn't budge. She was flung onto her back, barely managing to stop herself from ending up inside the bag once more. Scout returned and called out to Briella, wishing her friend had remained where she left her. Briella's head poked up over the edge of the bag as she lifted herself high enough for her wings to flap her to safety.

"What were you doing?" Scout scolded, zooming into the room with an irritated expression.

"Trying to close the bag. Surely, you should have known I would attempt to do this."

"Yes," Scout rested a hand on her hip. "I should have."

Briella became all business. "You go to that end," she pointed to the far side of the bag, "and grab the material where the zip is and pull backwards. That should help to pull the material taught so that I can slide the zipper closed."

"Okay," Scout agreed. Scout was impressed. Her idea was working like a charm. They managed to get the bag zipped halfway when they heard footsteps in the hallway. "Time to go," Scout shouted, holding her position until Briella had let go of the pull tab. She didn't want a repeat of earlier. They flew out the window and quickly found some kittens to play with. Snow was asleep, Stubs was off exploring somewhere, and Champ was annoying so that left Shadow and Ash.

Briella sauntered up to the kittens and said, "Want to play?"

"Sure," Shadow replied. "What did you have in mind?"

"I don't know," Briella admitted. "I thought you might know a game or two."

"Nope," Ash said. "We are babies. We are getting quite good at rough and tumbling each other, but we don't know how to play with an animal like you."

"We usually hunt and eat things like you," Shadow confessed.

"Well, that is definitely off the table," Scout said, clapping her hands together. "Would you be opposed to us riding you like a horse?"

"What do you mean?" Shadow asked.

"Let me show you," Briella answered, swinging herself up onto Snow's shoulders and scratching her behind the ears.

"You want us to carry you around?" Ash asked.

"For starters," Scout said, thinking how unskilled she was as a rider.

"Where is the fun in that?" she queried, although the pleasure on Snow's face made her think it might not be such a bad game after all.

"The real fun comes much later," Briella thought, picturing the jousting sticks she had hidden away in a drawer.

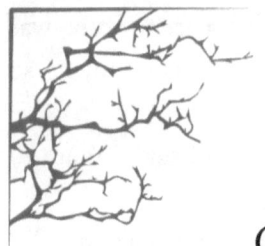

Chapter Seven

The skeleton waited until he was sure the fairies were gone. He was relieved that the person who had scared them had continued past his room. He wriggled around in the bag until he could get his bony fingers out from beneath his hips. He reached up and searched for the gadget that would ensure release from his current confinement. Accomplishing that task, he rolled over onto his side and then used his forearms to crawl his way out of the bag.

He squinted his eye sockets against the brightness of the light and shivered as the fresher air hit his frame. He trembled as he rose to his feet, taking a few moments to find his balance, the undertaking made more difficult without the presence of muscles but made possible through Briella's fairy dust. He stood still, as if listening to the whispering of his bones telling him what they required to work effectively. He slid his left foot forward, widely smirking as he kept his balance. Obviously, he couldn't smile in the conventional way because he would need flesh and skin to smile properly, but opening his jaws slightly gave the impression of smiling. The more he opened his jaws, the bigger the 'grin'. He repeated the action with his right foot, his confidence growing slowly.

He kept his feet still as he gently swung his arms backwards and forwards. Then he raised them up and to the side before taking a step back. His knee joints collapsed, and he went crashing to the floor. He lay quietly for a few seconds as he searched for any sore points. Not noticing any, he slowly got to his feet and proceeded to practise movement once more. He did this over and over until he was able to walk forwards and backwards fluidly.

The skeleton walked to the front door and reached for the handle. He turned the knob and pushed out. When that failed, he pulled in and was soon standing in the doorway. His jaw bones separated slightly as he stepped outside and made his way to the stairwell, which gave him some pause. He puzzled over its strange structure and hovered a foot in the air before allowing it to drop. He had not learned that the movement required the bending of the other knee, and he toppled forward. He came to a stop on the landing between the first and second floors.

He didn't scream due to the lack of vocal cords. The clanging of his bones was not loud enough to rise above the laughter coming from the bar and the music currently playing on the jukebox. He struggled to his feet, pleased once more that he refrained from sustaining any broken bones. The skeleton was beginning to think he was invincible. He heard some voices coming from below and wondered if it was wise for him to be seen. He didn't feel like company, so he did the only thing he could think to do. He pressed himself against the wall and remained as still as possible. The gentleman headed for the bathroom, spotted him anyway and laughed merrily. He called out to the barman, "So, the boss finally decided to get into the spirit of Halloween, did he?"

"Not likely," was the reply. The guy merely shook his head as he opened the door and stepped inside. The skeleton didn't wait around for him to return. He lay down on the floor and used his arms to pull himself down the remainder of the stairs. He sprung to his feet and attempted to sneak out the front door. A gasp to his left had him spinning his head in that direction.

His gaze landed on Callum's expression of recognition and disbelief. He realised his quest for freedom might very quickly end with his recapture. The skeleton decided to take a chance that his body would adapt swiftly to a faster pace without mishap. He increased his velocity and exited the building as Callum threw his napkin on the table and pushed his bowl filled with apple crumble and custard aside. He heard the scraping of chairs as the doors closed.

The area outside was very bright, and he struggled to find the right place to hide. Other than the parking lot, which was dotted with cars, the area around the pub was bare of structures. There wasn't any room beneath the pub for him to crawl into, so the vehicles became his only escape option. He sized up his chances and realised they were slim. His owner would reach him before he could climb in underneath.

He decided to run around the side of the building when a loud rumbling began to draw near. He thought he might scale the outside of the structure and hide out on the roof. When he saw the truck bearing down the road, with no intention of stopping although slowing down to the speed limit for a built-up area, he came up with another idea. He ran for the vehicle, not thinking of anything other than getting away. He didn't want to be stuffed back in the bag. He wanted to go home, to reunite with his family.

Callum ran as fast as he could, quickly followed by everyone else who had been in the dining area. They had witnessed him take off and wanted to see what had captured his attention. Glenvale was usually a quiet town, not a lot of mischief going on. However, these past few weeks had proven to be highly entertaining, if not terrifying, at the same time. As a result of his followers, Callum had to remain in his human form. The skeleton somehow managed to grab onto one of the vertical handles at the back of the truck and was dragged up onto a ledge. He smiled at Callum triumphantly as he held on for dear life.

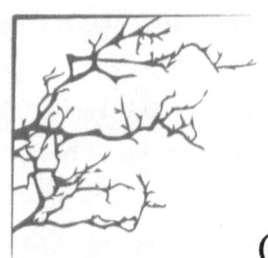

Chapter Eight

Callum sprinted towards the pub, refusing to answer any of the questions thrown his way. April and Force had an inkling that Briella's magic was at the centre of the drama but couldn't fathom how Callum factored into the scenario. They assured everyone the skeleton they saw was a trial run of a new gadget designed for the Halloween party by one of their friends. The excitement in the air as the patrons returned to their meals was palpable.

Force headed up the stairs after Callum leaving April to gather up the dessert plates. He arrived at April's door to find the room's occupants terrified by their companion's behaviour. Force stepped inside, "Callum, that's enough!" and then positioned himself between Callum and the fairies.

"They did something to my skeleton," Callum snarled angrily.

Briella seized Scout's hand, "I told you there were bones in there."

Callum pointed at her, "There, you see. Guilty as charged."

Force turned to Briella, "Why were you in Callum's bag?"

Briella hung her head in shame, "He said he'd brought a house-warming gift that would fit in perfectly with our party theme. With my magic on the fritz, I was worried about what that might be. I needed to know what was in there before the chaos associated with my magic reached its strongest peak."

Callum was furious. Not that the fairies had rifled through his stuff, but that his present had gotten up and run away. He had spent a great deal of time searching for that particular skeleton. He had wanted one that was scuffed up a little but not too old that it wouldn't suit his needs. There was not enough time to find another one to replace it.

"Why did you have to use magic on it?" he growled.

"It wasn't on purpose," Briella lifted her chin while crossing her arms across her chest.

"You can't leave well enough alone, can you? Can't have any surprises, can we?"

April entered, placing the plates in the fridge, and noticed the tension in the room.

Briella shook her head, knowing what was coming. Scout flew towards Callum, hoping to have a quiet word. She didn't make it in time. "I should have known what you'd do after taking a peek beneath that tablecloth."

Scout fumed, "Oh, you spiteful man."

The frown on April's face dropped as her sorrow became evident. "You viewed your new house without me?"

Briella dropped her head, but not before April saw the remnants of her guilt in her eyes. The feeling of betrayal that April felt was profound. "I very much wanted to be there when you saw it for the first time."

'I'm sorry," Briella said.

"I knew I should have stuck to the plan of assembling your new home at our new house. I was worried the pieces would become damaged if they travelled individually." April turned around, picked up her handbag and walked out the door. Briella flew after her, but Callum's thunderous advance stopped her in her tracks.

"How do I retrieve my skeleton?"

"I don't know," Briella admitted. "I did not create him. Therefore, he won't follow my instructions." She looked past him, but April was gone. Briella turned around and flew out the window.

Scout fluttered closer to him, "We'll find your skeleton and bring it home. Briella's magic will stop fuelling him at dawn. If we haven't seen him by then, he will at least be dormant." She turned on her heel and went in search of Briella.

Callum grabbed himself a glass of water and his bowl of dessert, and sat down on the couch. He put his feet up on the coffee table and casually sipped his drink. Force placed the kittens on the floor and opened some tins of kitten food. "Aren't you going to go out and look for your skeleton?"

"Nope," Callum replied.

"Then why bother carrying on like you did?" Force retrieved the can of cat food he had opened earlier from the fridge for the mother cat and gave her a small amount.

"The fairies are going to look for Skelly. If they don't return with him by nightfall, I will join in the search."

"He will be harder to find in the dark," Force stated. "You would have better luck looking now."

Callum merely smiled. "I am not wasting a beautiful day searching for something they let loose. It is their responsibility to return my property. What time is settlement on your property?"

Force consulted his watch. "April should be there by now and the keys should be changing hands as we speak."

"Right then," Callum said, getting to his feet. "Why don't we head on over to the house?"

"For what purpose?"

"You said the place needed a lot of work. We don't have a lot of time between now and Halloween to get the site ready for a horde of descending people. I've taken the liberty of organising some portable toilets. They should be arriving at 3pm. There will also be a crew of council workers arriving around that time to deliver some blockades. They should prevent your neighbours from witnessing our unique abilities as we prepare the landscape."

"How do you propose we explain away the swiftness of the erected structures?"

"You told me the people of this town have already concluded that you and April are very well connected. It would be stupid to discontinue developing that assumption for as long as you can," Callum shrugged.

"I guess," Force replied, pulling his mobile phone out of his pocket and bringing up April's number. He pressed the dial button and waited for her to answer. Callum eyed the device with dawning horror. Imagine if April had tried to ring Force when they'd been dining together earlier. She would have discovered Force's idea to pull a switcheroo on her. Callum wondered if April was the forgiving type. For Force's sake, he hoped so.

"She's already at the house," Force informed him after ending the call.

"You might want to swap phones with me," Callum said, holding out his hand.

Force's expression quickly mirrored Callum's as realisation set in. "Crikey," he breathed, handing over the phone.

"Dodged a bullet there," Callum replied, handing his phone over with the security code.

Force squinted his eyes, trying to figure out what else they had forgotten.

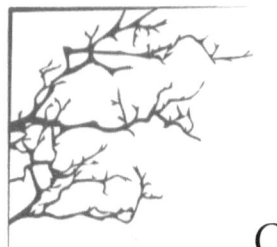

Chapter Nine

Skelly hung on for dear life as the truck careened down the road. He wondered how he managed to board the swiftly moving vehicle in the first place when he had been stumbling around since the moment he woke. Skelly concluded that he wouldn't fumble if he didn't worry too much over what he was trying to do.

He attempted to view the upcoming landscape a couple of times, but the windshear was too high. He was afraid of losing his head. Instead, he had to settle for his eye sockets roving over the countryside the truck had already passed. His spirits perked up when they came across a dirt road that split off from the highway. Three white pieces of wood shaped into an upside-down U had the words 'Glenvale Cemetery' written in a large black font.

He glanced at the bitumen, then wished he hadn't. Skelly took a leap of faith as he let go of the handle and sprung off the ledge. He landed on his feet but did not allow his knees to cushion the blow. He tumbled head over heels until finally coming to a stop in the middle of the road. He checked himself for breaks, relieved to find he had only dislocated a finger. He popped it into place and then backtracked to the cemetery's entrance.

Skelly barely missed being run over by a fast-moving vehicle that didn't see him until the last moment. The driver of the car swerved violently, blasting his horn furiously. Skelly stared at the car, the brake lights hypnotising him with their brightness. The driver threw open his door before jumping out of the vehicle. Skelly spun around and ran for the safety of the cemetery.

The guy couldn't believe his eyes. He ran for one hundred metres before his brain began questioning his decision to chase after a skeleton in the middle of nowhere, close to a cemetery. The guy seemed quite concerned as he mumbled to himself while high-tailing it back to his car. He threw the car into gear and slammed his foot on the accelerator, promising to abstain from drinking a couple of beers with his lunch in the future.

The sign loomed welcomingly over Skelly's head. Although he couldn't read a letter, the monuments that lay on either side of the road called to him like a moth to a flame. He wandered around the cemetery, searching for something that was out of reach. He wanted to be reunited with his family but didn't know his name, let alone those of his kin. He was simply counting on the universe to provide him with a sign that he had found his way home. Alas, the signal never came.

He spent a few hours caressing the different materials that made up the headstones and monuments. He was smart enough to hide behind them when people came to visit their loved ones but hastily resumed his quest the moment their taillights were no longer in view. Eventually, he deduced that he did not reside there and snuck into the back of an elderly gentleman's vehicle. When the car finally came to its resting point, Skelly waited a few minutes after the man had departed before taking leave himself. He opened the door, not the least bit surprised to find it unlocked, and became exasperated to find himself across the road from the pub.

Skelly swung his head from left to right, then turned his body ninety degrees and repeated the action. He searched desperately for a place to go. There was no way he was going back in the bag if he could help it. He spun around a few times and then chose to run in the direction he was facing. After a while, he established he had made the right decision. In no time at all, he came upon a group of buildings that reminded him of home.

This place felt right, deep inside his bones. He studied the fence made from chicken wire and framed by lumps of wood. It didn't look too hard to navigate. He took a run at it, placing his hands on top of the horizontal piece of wood and then swung his legs over. His right foot got caught in the wire, slamming his body into the fence on the other side. He hung upside down for a few minutes until he managed to unhook his toes, which led to him landing head-first in the dirt.

Skelly rose to his feet, shook off his clumsiness, and then walked towards the first building, to pause at the bottom of the stairs. It was much easier to walk up the steps than to come down them, he soon discovered. Curiosity had him quickly peering inside the first set of windows. Unable to find what he was looking for, he moved onto the next window frame. Skelly continued until he reached the end of the classroom.

Disappointment had him sitting on the veranda at the top of the staircase. Like a child beginning to learn how to manoeuvre himself, Skelly passed over each step on his bottom by moving his legs further down the stairs. He quickly moved to the next building, bouncing eagerly on the balls of his feet as he saw what lay beyond the windows of the first classroom.

An excited breath escaped him as he hurried to the door. He reached for the handle, becoming agitated when it refused to budge. He gripped the thing with both hands, pulling as hard as he could. He tried to move it up, and when that failed, he attempted to push it down. Silence remained as he opened his mouth to scream in frustration.

He couldn't even get the door to rattle. He searched the outside of the building and found a small rock lying on the ground. He picked it up and headed back to the door, where he pulled his arm back as far as it would go. Skelly flung his arm forward with tremendous force. The rock hit the glass and shattered it all over the floor on the inside of the room. Skelly's excitement grew more exuberant as he mouthed the word 'Home.'

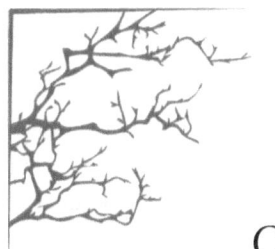

Chapter Ten

Scout was disappointed to find Briella trembling on top of Force's handlebars. She had hoped that her current emotional state would have allowed Briella to find the courage to traverse the open spaces in pursuit of April or the skeleton. To Scout's dismay, Briella had not managed to do that.

She landed beside her friend and made herself comfortable. Briella barely lifted her head in acknowledgement of Scout's arrival. With head hung low, she said, "Perhaps you should forget about being my friend, Scout. I only ever seem to get you into trouble."

Scout put her arm around Briella's shoulders. "No, you don't," she replied. "We've just had a couple of bumpy bits this week."

"This is going to continue to occur each year, Scout," Briella reminded her. "I'm just not sure how next year's drama will present itself."

"Let's worry about that then. Perhaps you should spend the couple of weeks leading up to Halloween here each year. Force will have the crystals in place, and you will be safe in our fairy garden once Force has built it. He will be able to supply you with the mushrooms you need if you run out, and there will always be a supply of flowering plants for your supply of nectar. I can keep an eye out in your area for those two weeks and keep the people safe while you stay here to take care of yourself."

Briella turned her head away, "Perhaps."

Scout was unconcerned. She had planted a seed that she hoped would germinate some positivity. "Any idea where the skeleton went?"

"Yep."

Scout scowled slightly, "Want to share?"

Briella flicked her head to the left. "He went that way."

Scout peered over her shoulder and frowned, "There is nothing of interest in that direction until you get to the next town. Why would he have gone that way?"

"He hitched a ride on the back of a truck," Briella stated, her tone conveying a touch of pride.

Scout shot to her feet, her wings flapping steadily, "He what? How are we going to find him?"

"He'll come back," Briella shrugged, unconcerned.

Scout was shocked by her response. "What makes you think that?"

"He wants to go home, wherever that is."

"How do you know that?"

Briella gave her *the look* – you know, the one that asks, 'Are you kidding me?' without having to say the words.

"Why would that make him come back here?"

48

"Callum is the only one who knows where he came from."

Scout appeared sceptical, "I still think we should look for him."

"Fine," Briella grumbled, getting to her feet. "I've got nothing better to do."

Scout rolled her hand over so the palm was facing up and then moved it in a sweeping motion, "After you."

Briella searched for the thin ribbon of energy that lingered behind. She picked it up near the entrance to the carpark. Briella pointed it out to Scout. Rather than following Briella's lead, Scout was now familiar with the signature and able to follow the ribbon. They followed it to the cemetery. The skeleton had been there for quite some time when the fairies finally made their entrance. They observed him from a distance, paying homage to every person laid to rest. A deep sadness befell the fairies as they witnessed his actions.

Scout turned to Briella her eyes glistening with unshed tears, "Do you think he is mourning the people lying there?"

"No," Briella said, clasping Scout's hand in her own. "He is searching for his family, but he doesn't know who he is. Poor thing doesn't know he is supposed to be an inanimate object."

"We should explain things to him so he doesn't feel so bad."

"Would you believe me if I said something like that to you?"

Scout scoffed, "Of course not. I am real."

"Are you really? How do you know that I haven't brought you to life so that I could have a friend my size? By morning, you could simply become a drawing of a fairy on a piece of paper." Briella returned her gaze to the skeleton, wishing she had never opened the bag.

Scout sat on the headstone with a stunned expression on her face. *'Am I real?'* she wondered.

The sound of an approaching car caused their bodies to stiffen. They looked around for somewhere to hide; however, the cemetery was devoid of trees or any other tall structures. There was not even a gazebo to shelter visitors from the elements. They looked on with fear as the car slowly passed. They released a relieved breath as the car continued forward. Scout chuckled, "I don't know why I was so concerned. Humans would not recognise us as fairies from that distance away. If they saw us at all, they would assume we were some sort of insect."

"Are you sure? The humans around here tend to take more notice of things than those living in the city."

"I am positive," Scout smiled gently. "I think I was picking up vibes from you. You can relax a little when you are here, Briella. You don't need to be on your guard so much here."

"You do remember what time of year it is?"

Scout patted Briella's hand. "Yes, because you keep reminding me. Your magic can't do much damage to them from here."

"I suppose you are right," Briella answered, her mind quickly turned to what lay beneath them. She shuddered violently, but thanks to Scout's calming words, her fairy dust remained contained within her body. Briella turned her attention back to the skeleton. She watched him peeking from behind his hiding place as an elderly gentleman sat on a wheelie walker talking to his dearly departed. The fairies assumed he was visiting his wife as they remained huddled closely together. They were surprised by the skeleton's actions. He crawled along the ground, keeping a watchful eye on the guy. He climbed in through the driver's door of the car and then crept into the back of the vehicle.

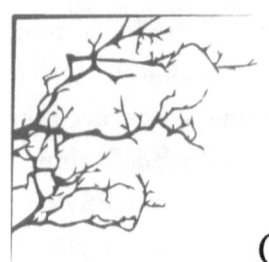

Chapter Eleven

Scout and Briella were no longer worried about being seen. They waited for the front of the car to pass them before heading for the rear bumper. They quickly settled themselves and then held on as tightly as possible without damaging their delicate skin on the sharp metal. "Where do you think we are going?" Briella shouted with a high degree of concern.

"Back to Glenvale," Scout replied confidently.

"Are you sure?"

"Yes. We are travelling back the way we came. Besides, I recognised the driver through the window. He is the local priest."

"So, that was not likely to be his wife back there then?" Briella queried.

Scout shook her head, "More likely, a parent or sibling."

"Where do you think he is taking us?"

"No idea, not that it matters. We came for the skeleton, which is currently in this car."

"I suppose so," Briella muttered; the idea of the unknown was frightful for her.

Her mood brightened considerably when the car slowed down and turned into a driveway. The driver parked the vehicle directly opposite the entrance to the pub. A thankful giggle escaped her.

"Happier now?" Scout smiled.

Briella nodded, a massive grin on her face. The priest stepped out of the car and meandered towards the front door. Briella's smile dropped as bewilderment took hold, "Doesn't anyone lock their doors around here?"

"You are in the country now, Briella. Everyone knows and trusts each other."

"Everyone?"

"Well, everyone except Loretta. She began locking her doors against intruders, and that was before Calamity went missing." Scout's eyebrows furrowed.

The sound of a door closing had the fairies fluttering towards the back windscreen. The skeleton was out and looking for somewhere to go. "We best follow him," Briella murmured.

Scout nodded her agreement. They waited for him to choose a direction, then followed in hot pursuit. The skeleton was fast for something that had barely learnt to walk. The fairies had no trouble keeping up with him. "I'm going to need a drink when he reaches his destination."

"Me too," Briella replied. "I hope there are some flowers nearby. All the rain puddles have dried up."

"You would drink out of a puddle?"

Briella rolled her eyes. "If I was thirsty enough. Which I am."

The fairies stopped talking to conserve their energy and prevent their mouths from feeling even drier. They landed on some port racks that supplied space for the students to store their bags while inside the classrooms. It also provided a barrier between the veranda's edge and the one-and-a-half-metre drop to the ground below. They hid behind a support beam, poking their heads out only as far as they needed to be able to see. "Look at his face, Briella. He appears to be happy."

Briella agreed, "Callum must have bought him from a school."

Scout seemed a bit perplexed, "Do schools usually sell their goods to the public?"

"I don't know," Briella shrugged. "But the skeleton certainly appears to be at home, don't you think?"

"Hmmm," Scout nodded thoughtfully. "Why don't you go and find something to drink? I'll stay here and keep an eye on him."

"Are you sure?"

Scout nodded. Briella didn't wait around to see if Scout would change her mind. She stayed close to the buildings and soon found what she was looking for, a lovely bunch of milkweed flowers. She drank her fill of the milky sap and headed back to Scout's position when the crash of breaking glass occurred. Briella changed course and soon discovered the skeleton had found a way inside the building that would not please the locals.

"April will have to pay for that," Briella glared.

"Nah, Force will fix it," Scout amended.

Briella raised an eyebrow. Scout grinned cheekily, "He knows he's got the hots for her now."

Briella's face rippled with the beginnings of a smile. "Yes, he does."

They flew to the windows and peered inside. They observed the skeleton moving between the rows of desks, searching for something. He opened cupboard doors and looked beneath the benches that rimmed the classroom. He moved to the far wall and opened another door. A gasp flew from their mouths as he stepped inside a small room and returned with a smaller version of himself. Briella turned to Scout, "He's found his family."

"It appears so," Scout agreed. Skelly shook the skeleton slightly and waited for a response. When he didn't receive one, he gripped the humerus more tightly and gave a more vigorous shake.

"Uh, oh," Briella groaned. "He's not going to be happy when the other one remains dormant. You'd better go and grab yourself a drink. I think you are going to need it."

Scout shook her head, "You need me here."

"I'll be fine for a couple of minutes. Off you go. Quickly now," she shooed Scout away.

When Scout returned, the skeleton was on the floor - face up. Skelly was giving it compressions. "You've got to be kidding me!" she muttered, placing her forehead in the palm of her hand.

"Do you have your phone with you?"

"No," Scout admitted reluctantly. Here was another moment when it would have come in handy to have it, and she had left it behind.

"That's a shame. Why don't you go and tell Callum that we've found his skeleton."

Scout considered the idea carefully. That would mean leaving Briella alone, where there was nobody to keep her fear and anger under control. Briella could release her magic, and they could potentially find themselves in a worse situation than they found themselves in before. On the other hand, Callum was furious with Briella. If he continued to criticize her, she would likely dose an innocent object with her contaminated magic.

"I think it would be best if you went and told him. It might help to mend the rift between you both."

"That might be the case, but I feel safer here than flying out there."

Scout was careful to keep the groan to herself. Briella was never going to be the fairy she was supposed to be. Her living in the country was never going to work. She was too used to city living, where there were multiple structures within easy reach to duck and hide behind. "I'll be back soon," she promised.

"We'll be here," she replied to Scout. *'I hope,' she said in her head.*

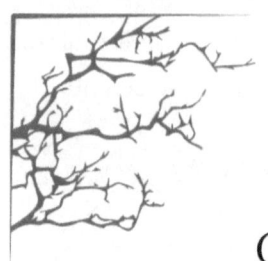

Chapter Twelve

Scout's capability for speed was high. She exuded maximum energy to produce the highest velocity she had ever achieved in her life. This surprised her, considering she was not being hunted.

She wasn't too concerned about her energy levels. She knew she had more than enough to get her where she needed to go, and there were plenty of mushrooms in the cupboard at her destination to offer replenishment. When she arrived at the pub, however, her trio of Gatherers was gone. They were nowhere to be found.

What was going on? They hadn't been gone that long, surely. Scout peered at the time on the clock. It seemed they had. She rushed over to the kitchen counter. Her phone was no longer there. "Damn!" She fluttered to the food cupboard, pleased to see the bag of mushrooms waiting for her. She didn't bother setting up an eating area; she merely sat on the cupboard floor and began breaking off suitable sizes of fungus to eat.

When she was almost full, she flew to the fridge and opened the door with a bit of help from her fairy dust. There was no way she was going inside without the benefit of a bit of dusting. She plucked a couple of blackberries out of their container and sucked out the juice before throwing the husk away. She didn't want to fly on a full stomach, which would slow her down. Scout now had a lot further to travel as the Gatherers were most likely at the new house, and Force had relocated her phone.

Scout didn't recognise the place when she got there. Tall plastic structures barricaded the area around the house. Funny-looking buildings lined four blocks in groups of three. These, she would later come to discover, were portable toilets for their guests. Large plastic sheets wrapped the outside of the newly erected scaffolding that bordered the house.

April, Force and Callum stood around the far side of the house. They were inspecting a cat aviary that Force had knocked up to keep the kittens safe until after the party. Michelle, Paul, Geoffrey and Jacinta were standing beside them, marvelling over his craftsmanship.

Paul eyed the structure dubiously, "You've only had the cats for two days?"

"Yep," Callum replied, pretending to be Force.

Paul wandered around the massive, multi-storeyed structure, "You managed to build this from scratch in that time."

"I had some help," he glanced at April, who hid a smile.

"You two did this?" his voice rose an octave. Feeling quite embarrassed, he cleared his throat.

April tucked her hands behind her back and crossed her fingers, "We had some help from our friends, Paul. Colleagues who gave up some of their off-duty time to give us a hand. They've been here all afternoon, helping us out."

She wished the four of them would leave. It was lovely that they were willing to be so helpful and all. Still, it was detrimental to have to tamper with their minds continually. The Gatherers didn't have the time to wait for their neighbours to go home before beginning their preparations. They also didn't have 'friends' who could come and give them a hand. Nor did they need them. They simply didn't know how to ask them to leave without hurting their feelings or having to plant another suggestion in their minds. Scout soon fixed that problem.

She projected her thoughts at Force only, *'Where's my phone?'*

He answered her through mind-link once he realised the other two hadn't heard her. *'In the top drawer of the bedside table situated in the primary bedroom on the left-hand side as you walk in.'*

Scout retrieved her phone quickly and used it to ring him. "I've found him, Force. He's at the school."

"I'm sorry, who is this?" Callum asked, confusion lacing his voice.

"Oh, it's you Callum. It's me, Scout."

"How can I help you, Nancy?"

"Do you want me to repeat what I said, Callum, or did you hear me the first time?"

Callum turned away from their guests, a mischievous grin on his face. "I'm not sure if I am able to offer assistance at this time. Would you like the number of a colleague?"

Scout hung up in his ear. Callum chuckled softly. "Yes, that sounds like something that requires investigation."

Paul shuffled his family together, "Sounds like another case. We best be off." He turned to April, "We'll leave you to it."

April nodded, "Thanks for your help. We appreciate it very much."

Geoffrey stepped forward, "I can stay and lend a hand."

"Thanks, Geoffrey, but that is not necessary. We would love for you to give us a hand fixing up the house the way we want it after Halloween. Are you still okay with that?"

"You bet," he replied happily.

Force and April walked hand in hand as they escorted the Tillies to the front of the house. Callum remained out the back, continuing his conversation on a disconnected line until he was sure they were out of earshot. Then, he searched the device for the list that displayed the most recent calls and selected Scout's number. He listened to the ringtone right up until the phone diverted to the message bank when he ended the call. "Two can play at this game," he growled aggressively.

With the school's name placed into the search bar of the phone's navigation system, Callum soon had a map to refer to for directions. He memorised the layout within seconds, then transformed himself into a green and yellow budgerigar and flew away. April and Force returned to the back of the property to discover he had disappeared.

"Where did he go?" she asked.

"I'm not sure," Force replied, spotting the glowing screen in the grass. *What are you up to, Callum?'* he wondered, retrieving the device and inspecting the display. He turned it around so April could view the map.

"Why would Liam be headed for the school?" she queried with a frown.

Force closed the app and retrieved the details of the last phone call. "Scout contacted him."

"The girls must have found the skeleton."

"And he's gone to retrieve it."

"Why wouldn't he wait for you? It is your skeleton, after all."

"Why indeed?" Force replied.

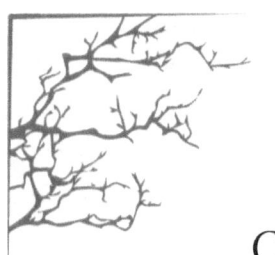

Chapter Thirteen

No matter how hard Skelly tried to revive his new friend, every action he put into effect was unsuccessful. He became concerned when a slight glow became visible across his body. He wondered if it had something to do with the skeleton that was lying on the floor. Was it trying to steal some of his life force?

Unprepared to take the risk, Skelly rose to his feet, placing his hands on his hips while he searched for a suitable place for his buddy to rest. He certainly wasn't going to be cruel enough to leave it lying on the floor. Nor was he interested in putting it back inside the cupboard. More than anything, Skelly was disappointed to discover he would not find out whether his new friend was male or female.

His eye sockets came to rest on the chairs that sat atop the students' desks. He strode to the front of the room and then grabbed the chair situated in the middle of the front row. He placed it on the floor behind the desk, allowing enough room to position his new friend's frame comfortably. He soon discovered the chair was not tall enough to offer support to the skeleton's upper body.

Skelly shook his head. This simply wouldn't do. He perused the room once more, sneering when he spotted the teacher's desk with the high-backed chair. Skelly gathered up his friend and moved him to his new resting place. He appraised his handiwork and concluded it was good. A glance to the right revealed the sun was getting low in the sky. He didn't want to be alone in the dark, so he walked out the door and slowly made his way down the stairs.

Briella jumped to her feet, unsure of what to do. Scout had not yet returned with reinforcements. If she left with the skeleton, there would be no way for her to help Scout track their movements. If Briella let him go, they may not be able to find him again. She tapped a finger on one of the railings while she considered the ramifications of her options. Her head hung low, and a scowl was plastered firmly on her face.

Coming to a decision, Briella scanned the area between the two buildings to locate his latest position. Her eyes widened considerably when they noticed the soft glow that illuminated his body. A feeling of deep satisfaction came over her when she realised they would be able to find him quickly in the darkness. No longer afraid of losing anybody, Briella sat down on the rail and waited for Scout's arrival. The skeleton peered at her over his shoulders, fixing her with an intensely intimate stare. She shivered, her legs discontinuing their swinging action. At the same time, her mind worked furiously to determine whether he could be aware of her presence.

THE SNEAKY SKELETON

The skeleton tapped a finger to his forehead, pulling a gasp from the fairy. Skelly turned his head towards the gap between the buildings that moments ago had contained the last traces of the setting sun. Twilight had fallen, and very soon, the landscape would be in complete shadow. He returned his gaze to Briella, raised his hand and wiggled a finger at her. She jumped to her feet, harrumphing her displeasure at his action. She fluttered towards him, anger emanating from her pores.

She was unsure what his response implied. She assumed it was to indicate she'd been naughty or that she was not to follow him. How dare he make her happiness slip away, to be replaced by anger? Who did he think he was? Well, she wasn't having it. She flew for him, ready to give him a piece of her mind.

Skelly threw his head back, his body jerking with silent laughter. He managed to gather himself seconds before Briella reached him and ran for the fence line at the other end of the compound. He scaled the fence quickly, moving on instinct rather than rational thought. This had proved to be instrumental in ensuring he did not trip over his own feet. Skelly landed on the other side without incident and ran for the trees in the distance.

He tried not to think about the radiance of his bones. His main priority was to lose the fairy. Only then would he be able to consider the task of extinguishing the glow that coated his frame and provide some protection from the view of those probing eyes. The issue at hand seemed to be – how to ditch the fairy with his body lit up like a jack-o-lantern.

Skelly never slowed when reaching the edge of the forest. He dashed inside with Briella hot on his trail. She scolded him for treating her with contempt when she was the one who had brought his inert skeleton to life. Skelly peered over his shoulder. What wouldn't he give for the ability to speak? The things he would say to this annoying diminutive creature. Well, it would be sure to make you blush. He weaved around the tree trunks but fell numerous times when his feet became tangled in the underbrush. Briella had no trouble navigating her surroundings. She flew close enough to Skelly's body that the light showed obstacles that could be harmful to her long before she reached them.

Another vine reached out and wrapped itself around his foot, bringing him down noisily. Briella winced at the sound. That had to have hurt a lot. She was careful not to get close enough for him to pluck her from the air when she flew down low to check on him. She reached out a hand towards him, "Are you okay?"

He raised his head until his focus landed on her and nodded his head once. "Yes," he mouthed the word. She fluttered a little higher, watching him closely for any sign he was about to make a sudden move. He gave no indication of moving at all.

"Do you want some help?" Briella asked, feeling responsible for his predicament.

Skelly shook his head slightly, slowly moving into a seated position. He wished to be left alone so that he could locate his family, who must be out of their minds with worry over him. His instincts told him that this fairy was harmful to his cause. He needed the other one. However, the knowledge required to remove this fairy from the equation and then locate the other was way beyond his comprehension.

"I'm happy to stay here with you until the sun rises. Would you like that?"

"No," he mouthed, his frame stiffening in response to the deep voice that broke the silence.

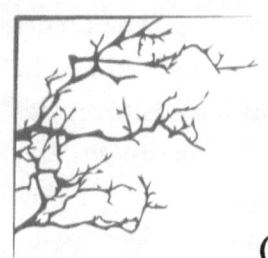

Chapter Fourteen

Briella jerked with surprise. She fluttered back a few centimetres, suddenly afraid of the creature that knelt before her. She peered at him intently, searching for evidence that his body had begun to grow a voice box. She nearly fell out of the sky when a beam of light suddenly appeared. When the voice spoke again, she realised it belonged to one of the Gatherers.

"There's my good skeleton. Come along now. Time to go home."

"Oh, it's you, Callum," Briella breathed a sigh of relief. *"I thought the skeleton had learned how to talk."* She giggled quietly, just loud enough for her ears alone.

"I'll take it from here," he said. "You may leave."

"What do you mean?" she fluttered towards him. *"Where is Scout?"*

"I don't know," he said, leaning down to grab hold of Skelly's arm. Skelly jerked to his feet but was too slow to avoid Callum's grip. He yanked his arm as hard as he could, but Callum stood firm. Skelly was determined to remain free. There was no way he was going back inside that bag. He allowed himself to be dragged a couple of metres before digging his heels into the dirt and leaning away from his captor.

Although his frame weighed next to nothing, he surprised Callum with his sudden act of resistance. Callum stumbled slightly yet didn't let go of his prize although his grip slid down to Skelly's hand. He snorted rather loudly as he tightened his grip and surged forward. There was a loud popping noise as Skelly's hand came free of his wrist. Callum fell forward while Skelly tumbled backwards.

Not one to waste an opportunity, Skelly launched to his feet and scrambled further into the woods. Expletives poured out of Callum's mouth as he took off after his skeleton. Briella rushed after them, afraid of being left alone in the dark. Skelly successfully weaved around obstacles in his path for a good ten minutes before the ground fell away beneath him, and he belly-flopped into the creek.

A silent scream thrust his mouth open. His arms thrashed about, finding resistance beneath the water. He expected a hand to come down and yank him from his watery grave. None was forthcoming. When something bumped into his skull, he realised that there was a current in the stream. He kicked his legs and swished his arms, hoping to reach the surface rather than the riverbed.

With panic starting to kick in, he finally breached the surface, only to find himself sinking to the depths below when his legs ceased to move. His mouth hung open as he struggled to resurface. Once he'd succeeded, Skelly continued to kick like crazy until he bumped into the shoreline.

He reached out with his remaining hand and hung on for dear life as the current threatened to wash him away. Skelly worked his way up the length of the tree root with great difficulty until his upper body rested comfortably upon the riverbank. Though he didn't need to catch his breath, his shoulders rose and fell with the upheaval. To his dismay, the glowing of his bones had not diminished at all.

Skelly scrambled away from the edge of the river and carefully made his way downstream. He had no idea of his destination but knew he would only find what he sought by continuing to move forward. It took him two hours to find evidence of another living soul, a building in the distance that signalled like a lighthouse. He observed the lights as they winked on and off in the different areas of the house. He wondered at the cause of such a phenomenon and decided to have a closer look.

He dashed across the meadow with great haste and much fear. The moon hung large in the sky, and the light reflected from its surface was almost as bright as him. Although a distant howl created a shiver in his bones, he could not discern any voices in the vicinity. Skelly's head whipped around in a constant search for danger. He had almost made it to the back of a humungous shed when the back door to the house opened, and a young blonde girl stepped into view.

Skelly witnessed her slight hesitation from the soft glow of the porch light before continuing on her way down the stairs. Her footsteps picked up in pace once she'd reached the final tread, and by the time she was close enough to realise something was amiss, she was practically running. She slowed her gait as she said, "I'm sorry. I thought you were William or Donovan."

Skelly shook his head. He was sure he was neither of those people.

"I can see that," Jacinta said, curiosity overriding her fear. "What are you?"

Skelly was looking around for a weapon he could use for protection. Jacinta took a step forward. "Your costume is amazing. You look as though you truly are a skeleton. Where did you get it from?"

Skelly took a few steps to the left, and Jacinta mirrored him. Skelly peered over his shoulder. Though he did not wish to retrace his route, he didn't want to get captured by the girl either. She eyed him critically, "You know what would make your costume even better? A cloak and a scythe. Wait here. Dad has a cape that I think would fit you perfectly. I'm sure he would be happy to lend it to you until after Halloween. I'll be back in a flash," she called over her shoulder as she sprinted away.

He wasn't sure what to do. He hopped from one foot to the other before deciding to hide beneath the stairs. The flapping of wings had him squeezing himself in behind a hot water system housed under there. He didn't mind the tiny space as it shielded most of his body from view. He puffed out his chest as though taking a deep breath when he heard the door slam closed above him.

He watched her feet tread confidently on each stair as she made her way down. Watching her from that angle, he still couldn't work out where he had gone wrong. He noticed the disappointment that laced her voice as she asked him where he'd gone. The girl threw the cape, which landed on something he couldn't see. It hung in the air as though filled by a ghost.

She wandered over to the shed and pulled on the door. She turned on her torch and disappeared from view. Skelly moved cautiously from his hiding spot. Once he determined it was safe, he hurried over to the cape and snatched it up in his hand. He discovered she had hung it over a piece of wire that had been strung between two pieces of wood a few metres apart.

Skelly quickly worked out how the cloak should be worn and managed to put it on before the girl reappeared. He glanced down the length of his arms, thrilled to discover the glow that surrounded his body was no longer visible. He tucked his hand inside the sleeve, noting the only part of him that was visible to the public was his feet. He had time to find something to fix that problem now that he knew what he needed.

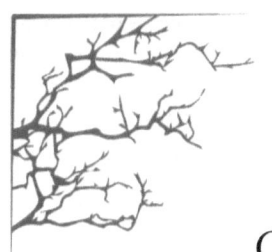

Chapter Fifteen

The skeleton dumbfounded Callum by getting away. He stood on the riverbank with Skelly's hand securely in his own as he attempted to peer beneath the murky water. The torchlight was no help at all. He turned to Briella and admitted he felt a bit of pride that the skeleton he had chosen as a gift had turned out to be highly resourceful and intelligent. Briella smiled; she was happy that Callum no longer intended to blame her for something she evidently had no control over.

"What do we do now?" she asked cautiously.

"We walk downstream to see if we can find him. He will come out of there sooner or later."

"How will we know where that is?"

"Hopefully, we will see him exit. Otherwise, we could be looking all night without success."

"I'm very sorry, Callum."

"What's done is done, Briella. Want to catch a ride? I suppose with your magic the way it is, you are as blind as a bat in the dark?"

"You would be right with that assumption," she admitted. "I would be grateful for your help."

"Would you still be happy if I were to transform into an owl?"

"As long as you don't want to eat me for dinner."

"Let me tell Liam we are going to conduct an aerial search."

"Why don't you tell him we've got this? Scout, Liam and April don't need to help us look, do they?"

Callum smiled, "You wouldn't be trying to play matchmaker, would you?"

"Who? Moi?" she giggled.

Callum reached into his pocket, but the phone wasn't there. "Oops," he muttered.

"You've got that right!" April's voice rang loud and clear.

"April," Callum and Force voiced together. Liam reached for her, but she moved out of his reach.

"It all makes sense now," she remarked. Her hands went to the chain around her neck, looking for the clasp.

Liam lurched towards her and captured her wrists in his hands. "Don't," he pleaded.

"Get off me!" she snarled with clenched teeth.

"The necklace is yours to keep, no strings attached. I bought it for you because it matches your eyes, and I knew that it would not only look great on you but that you would love it."

She struggled against his hold. "How stupid do you think I am?"

"What do you mean?" Force pulled her up against his body and wrangled her arms behind her back.

"I knew you and Callum had switched places from the very beginning. I can't believe you thought I was stupid enough not to notice." April struggled to free herself from his hold. She was not yet ready to use her powers against him. "Have you forgotten that as a Gatherer, I am able to detect an imposter when I see one? Especially since I have worked with you so often and know you so well?"

Force groaned softly, "When you didn't say anything, I thought Callum had managed to do the impossible."

April's struggles lessened slightly, "How could you of all people do that to me?"

He didn't exert any more pressure than was necessary to keep her still long enough to whisper the answer in her ear. "Because I don't want his lips on yours, *ever*. Don't ask me to apologise for my actions because I won't."

April's heart skipped a beat. The underlying emotion emanating from Force as he spoke those words spooked her immensely. She gritted her teeth harder, almost to the point of cracking her molars. "I want a divorce!" she cried defensively, fearful of the feelings that were blooming in her heart.

"Fine," he replied, letting her go. "Come on, Scout," he called over his shoulder as he began to walk away.

Not wanting to be left alone in the dark, she flew after him. "Are you coming, Briella?"

"No, I am going to stay and help Callum find his skeleton."

"Are you sure?" she asked with raised eyebrows.

"Yes. I've got to go and find him. He already has a huge head start."

April nodded, "You go. I'll be fine." She wrapped her arms around her midriff and walked to the water's edge. Callum shouted a warning, shining the torchlight upon the murky surface. April's steps faltered as she thanked him and then shooed them away. Callum transformed into a barn owl and waited patiently for Briella's decision.

He knew the girls were close, and he wondered if Briella was still willing to help him find the skeleton when April so obviously needed a friend. Respecting April's wish to be alone, Briella reluctantly landed on Callum's shoulders and positioned her legs so they would not interfere with his wingspan. Then she held on tightly as he launched into the air.

Callum followed the creek's layout without too much trouble, the dappled moonlight increasing the effectiveness of his enhanced eyesight. He did a couple of passes over the area between the site where Skelly went into the creek and the district three counties over before their eyes came to rest on Skelly's frame. Callum banked sharply to the right at the moment Briella began to point excitedly. He landed on the gutter of a building where they could observe the skeleton undetected.

If Skelly had noticed his landing, he gave no indication. He did seem to be searching for something; his head whipping from side to side. They wondered what he was doing when a door closed below them. Callum jumped slightly at the sound, his head twisting sharply to see what had created the noise.

From his position, he couldn't see anything. His focus returned to Skelly, who had frozen on the spot. Callum stood a little higher, becoming concerned when Briella made a strangled noise in her throat. He searched for the frequency that would allow him to link with Briella. She shouted her thoughts at him, making the task a lot easier. "Is that Jacinta?" Callum couldn't say. He was too busy watching where he was flying to take notice of the girl's features. Briella continued as though she was not asking him for an answer, "That girl has got rocks in her head. Who in God's creation is not frightened of a living, breathing skeleton? It's time somebody had a serious conversation with that girl. I'll have to have words with Force."

Callum's momentary glance picked up that Jacinta talked to the skeleton as though conversing with one of her friends. He had to admit, if only to himself, that the girl had guts. Even when Skelly went to go around the girl, she matched his movements. He nearly fell off his perch when she turned her back on him and made her way back to the shed. He almost choked on his spit as he spoke with Briella. *What is with this kid?*

Briella sighed, her hands ruffled his feathers, *"Jacinta has been earmarked to become a Battle Star."*

"By whom?"

"Force, originally. Guardian Karah agreed."

They watched the skeleton run towards the house and then disappear from view. *"Hold on,"* Callum cautioned as he took to flight, landing on the roof of the shed. They watched Jacinta return and the subsequent theft of the cloak. *"What is he up to?"*

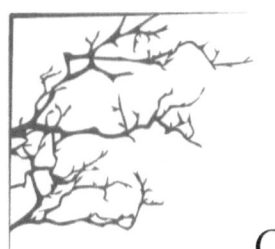

Chapter Sixteen

Callum expected Skelly to leave the area quickly. He was surprised once again by the skeleton's actions.

They followed his feet as he worked his way towards the house. The glow of his bones appeared to blink, similar to lights draped casually around a Christmas tree. Callum sharpened his gaze in an attempt to discover the cause of the strange phenomenon. It took him a few minutes, but Callum correctly determined that Skelly was attempting to walk in a squatting position so that the bottom of the cape hid his feet from view.

Skelly took a few steps, then paused for a few seconds to look over his shoulder before repeating the process. Callum wondered what Skelly was trying to accomplish. He was frustrated by his inability to converse with the skeleton and wished that Briella's magic had enabled the skeleton to communicate with him. Skelly finally reached the bottom of the staircase when Jacinta reappeared. She hurried from the shed, her arms heavily ladened with Halloween props and her view profoundly impaired. She nearly face-planted a couple of times but managed to remain on her feet. With each stumble, her load became a little lighter.

A grin spread across Skelly's face as he realised her predicament. His eyes took in the steepness of the staircase. He concluded that while Jacinta had difficulty seeing what was right in front of her, she would have no issues detecting movement from above. He ducked in under the steps and squeezed himself behind the hot water system once more.

"What are you up to?" Callum wondered.

Briella picked up on his projected thought and replied with, *"Only time will tell. How long are you planning on keeping an eye on him?"*

"Depends on how entertaining he is."

"He will become dormant at Dawn," she reminded him.

"Then let's hope the girl doesn't keep him in hiding for too long."

Skelly figured that it would take Jacinta a few minutes to deposit her load before returning for the fallen items. He waited until her feet were halfway up the stairs before leaving his hiding place. His feet touched the bottom rung the moment hers had reached the back door. He scaled the steps quickly, then searched the landing for some camouflage for his feet. Skelly found a substantial collection of shoes of varying styles in four different sizes. He chose a pair of black galoshes that fitted him perfectly in length but were loose around the middle. He had begun to retrace his steps when Geoffrey, Jacinta's newly adopted older brother, appeared at the doorway.

Skelly froze in place, his face fully bared to the newcomer. Geoffrey stopped in his tracks, his hand flying to his chest as a gasp left his lips. Within moments, deep belly laughs filled the air. "Awesome," he said, smacking his chest a couple of times. Geoffrey stepped forward to view the skeleton better. "It's a good thing you don't cackle like the witch Dad brought home, or I'd be standing in a puddle right now. Your eye sockets are so creepy. It's a pity they don't glow."

Geoffrey turned away from Skelly and headed down the stairs. Skelly remained frozen until Geoffrey had collected the dropped items and returned to the house. When he was sure the boy was gone, he raced down the stairs, stumbling a few times with his newly acquired footwear, and then headed for the road. He walked towards town, wishing that clouds would gather to provide him with some extra cover.

Callum stretched his wings and took flight. He was careful to remain in a position that his shadow wouldn't give him away. A car approached with its lights on high beam. The skeleton turned his back to the vehicle and tipped his head to the left. He brought his arms up so that his body made a cross and stayed completely still until the car had disappeared into the distance.

Briella dug her heels into Callum's body and pushed up with her knees. *"Will you take a look at that?"* she giggled. *"He looks like a scarecrow."*

"I think that is what he intended," Callum agreed.

"Where would he have learnt to do that?"

81

"I'm sure I ran past one when I was chasing him earlier."

"Really? What an ingeniously sneaky skeleton," Briella replied.

"Indeed," Callum agreed with an admiring tone. *"Mind you, it's not that hard to pull one over on humans."*

"You are right about that."

Lost in their conversation, they weren't paying attention to what they were seeing. Skelly's hand moved below the sleeve's edge. It rose in the air for a few seconds, then swung backwards, only to rush forward as though throwing some kind of weapon. The hand disappeared beneath the sleeve again as tiny spots of fluorescent yellow appeared in an arc ahead of him. Callum pulled up in the air, his wings swiftly flapping as he tried to determine what he had witnessed. He was wracking his brain for an explanation when Briella said, *"Are those Skelly's teeth?"*

"They couldn't possibly be," he replied, not wanting to believe what was right in front of him. *"Why would he do such a thing?"*

"Who knows?" Briella shrugged, feeling quite confused. Skelly was beginning to look more like a psycho than a sneaky skeleton. *"Where did he go?"*

Callum spun his head from one direction to another. He couldn't spot any sign of glowing bones or deeper shadows that would indicate the whereabouts of his skeleton. Everything fell into place. Clever skeleton. He had managed to distract Callum enough that even with the enhanced vision from being in the form of an owl, he could not locate his latest position. *"Damned if I know. He must have known we were following."*

"Well, your wings are loud enough," she admonished unintentionally. *"If you wait a minute, that bit of cloud will move away from the moon, and the ground will lighten considerably."*

Callum looped around and swooped, hoping the lower altitude would help the search. It did not. He couldn't find his skeleton anywhere, though he did spot Jacinta and her brother running through their backyard. "Do you suppose…?" he mused fleetingly before being cut off by Briella's thoughts. *"Oh, look at that. Geoffrey and Jacinta are playing chasey, and at this time of night."*

"I guess that is that then," Callum's mood deflated. He was looking forward to seeing what the skeleton would get up to in the wee hours of the morning. He flapped his wings faster and headed back to the pub. He would mount a search in the morning for the skeleton's lifeless body.

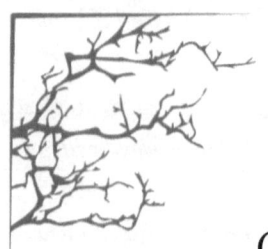

Chapter Seventeen

Geoffrey walked inside the house with a wide grin on his face. He placed the items on the kitchen table and then said to Jacinta, "Did you wet your pants when you spotted the reaper on the veranda?"

Jacinta frowned at him, "What do you mean?"

Geoffrey hesitated slightly, then said with a little less confidence, "The reaper outside."

"Oh," Jacinta replied, nodding her head while moving closer to the door. "The guy in the skeleton suit. I lent him Dad's cloak from the shed." The tapping of her finger on her thigh matched the rhythm of her footsteps. "I'm a bit surprised he came upstairs. Did he say anything to you?"

"Nope," Geoffrey shook his head. "Just stood there in a really creepy way. It was so cool. I thought he was a prop."

Paul walked into the kitchen and headed for the cupboard containing the glasses. He reached for the handle and said, "What prop are you talking about?"

Geoffrey and Jacinta answered simultaneously, "The skeleton."

Paul seemed confused as he grabbed a glass and stepped toward the sink. "We don't have a skeleton this year, kids. It got chewed up by Buster last Christmas, and we haven't gotten around to replacing it."

"Buster?" Geoffrey questioned.

Jacinta answered, "Our dog. He got bitten by a snake in March and died."

"I'm so sorry," Geoffrey stated.

Jacinta shrugged off the sadness by considering their conversation. "Who do you suppose is inside the costume?"

It was Geoffrey's turn to shrug his shoulders. "Beats me."

Paul filled his glass with water, took a sip, and then faced his kids. "Force's brother was complaining earlier about his skeleton running away. He was quite concerned as it is a prototype and very top secret. Perhaps it was his skeleton that you saw." Jacinta's grin sent chills down Paul's spine. "Don't you even think about it," he warned as she ran out the door.

"It could still be here," she called over her shoulder. "Better give Force a call and tell him to hurry up before the skeleton disappears again."

Paul placed his glass on the table and headed for his phone. He knew there was no point in trying to stop Jacinta from going after the skeleton. That girl had a mind of her own, and there was no stopping her when she got an idea into her head. He looked at Geoffrey and flicked his head. Geoffrey got the hint and followed Jacinta out the door.

He hurried down the stairs and jogged to her position before falling into step with her. Her head constantly moved as she tried to find the skeleton. "Do you see him?" she asked.

"No," he replied, looking everywhere himself. "He can't have gotten far."

"You wouldn't think so," Jacinta remarked, hoping Geoffrey was correct in his assumption. "There," she pointed to a spot by the road.

Geoffrey followed her outstretched arm, wondering what on Earth he was seeing. Small glowing objects were flying through the air. "What the?"

Jacinta squinted, keeping her eye on the shadow that was a bit darker than its surroundings. "Gotcha," she muttered triumphantly and ran in the skeleton's direction. Geoffrey swiftly followed, ducking his head as an owl suddenly swooped towards him. By the time he raised his head, Jacinta had considerably lengthened the gap between them. He wanted to ask her to wait up but was feeling out of breath. The six months the Jealousy Monsters had locked him up had taken their toll on his body, and it would take a little while longer for him to regain his strength and stamina. Instead, he kept his eye on her and tried to keep the distance between them short enough that he could maintain her in his sight.

The owl did another loop, swooping low and then maintaining the height as it glided through the air.

Geoffrey indicated his fright with a quiet squeak. He hated birds, especially when their wings flapped near his head, and their beak made those snapping sounds. Though his steps faltered, he did not stop in his pursuit of Jacinta. His mood brightened significantly when Jacinta suddenly veered to the left. Changing course himself, he realised he would soon catch up to her and ask her to stop running. Then he noticed the darkened shape running just ahead of her.

"Well, what do you know?" he thought. *"Jacinta found him and is tracking him."* Geoffrey was impressed by her skills. He could now see how she had helped Force and April find the missing children. Geoffrey decided he should not only be nicer to her than he had been already but that he should see if she were willing to teach him how to become more observant. He figured not allowing his mind to wander would help greatly when Jacinta suddenly launched herself into the air for seemingly no good reason. Had he been paying attention, he might have noticed the skeleton was about to jump across a stream that was extremely close to a thicket of trees. She took him down like a professional, leaving Geoffrey to once again marvel at her skills.

"Gotcha!" she cried victoriously, giggling endearingly.

Skelly bucked beneath her body, but she held on tightly to her catch. Geoffrey reached them, panting like a steam train now that he had stopped running. "Well done!" he exclaimed.

Jacinta looked up, grinning like a cat that had got the cream. "Give us a hand, will you?" she asked Geoffrey, only slightly out of breath. He grabbed Skelly beneath the left arm while Jacinta gripped the right. Together, they heaved the skeleton to his feet. Jacinta marvelled at the structure of the arm beneath the coat. It felt like a regular plastic skeleton found in novelty stores. "You, my new friend, are coming home with us. I don't know how much money you are worth, but I'm betting it's a lot. Force's brother is going to be so relieved to have you back into his care."

"I wonder how it works?" Geoffrey mused aloud.

"We'll figure that out when we get home." She assured him. Skelly walked beside them without a struggle. Jacinta wondered why he was being so accommodating when they had just chased him across the paddock. Little did she know how much the word 'home' meant to the skeleton.

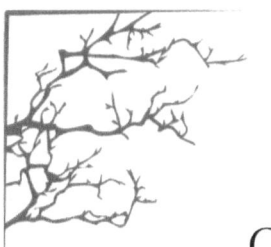

Chapter Eighteen

Paul and Michelle marvelled over the skeleton while they waited for him to be collected. While Jacinta and Geoffrey had looked everywhere for an on/off switch, they were unable to locate its whereabouts. Skelly spent the time wandering through the house, opening and closing doors, cupboards, and windows.

He became agitated when Force arrived but quickly quieted when it became apparent that he was going home. Skelly graciously climbed into the back of April's car and sat tranquilly on the seat. When the car started to move, he played with the door and window buttons. Nothing happened. Force had the forethought to kiddie lock the doors and windows before putting Skelly in the car. He rose onto his knees and peered out the rear window, but soon became bored and sat properly on the seat once more to stare out the side window.

When they reached the pub, he put up some resistance in getting out of the car. Callum was there to lend a hand, and the men had him up the stairs and contained inside their room in no time at all. Briella was relieved to see his bony frame. She hovered in front of him, just out of reach. "It's good to see you home. I was worried about you," she admitted.

Skelly didn't respond. He merely stood there with his arms at his sides. She tipped her head sideways, "I have to admit, I am a little surprised by the calmness you are displaying. I would have thought you would be itching to escape the moment they got you out of the car."

Callum gave a short cough, "Don't give him any ideas!"

Scout fluttered into the room, "Oh, you found him. How wonderful."

Briella hovered beside her friend. "His hand is still missing, though," she uttered sadly. "What happened to the boots and cloak?"

"I left them with Paul and Michelle. They offered us the use of the garments to hide our 'toy' from the community. I didn't see the need, so I declined their offer," Force replied.

"Fair enough," Briella said. "Shall I see if I can find his hand?"

Callum shook his head, "Don't bother. He's not much of a skeleton without teeth."

Force reached inside his jacket pocket, "I almost forgot. Geoffrey gave me these." He held his hand above Callum's and dropped the contents onto the Gatherer's palm.

Callum chuckled softly. "Thank you, brother."

Force returned the smile. "April's got some glue in the other room."

"Sweet," Callum replied, taking a step in that direction.

He glanced back at Skelly. "Might be an idea to secure him first."

"Indeed," said Force, walking into his bedroom and returning with a set of handcuffs. He placed one around Skelly's wrist and then motioned for the skeleton to follow him. He walked him into the bathroom, where he secured the other around the pipe beneath the basin. "That ought to hold you for a while."

Briella fluttered in the doorway, "I'll keep my eye on him."

Force raised an eyebrow, "I don't think so, love. Best you come with us."

Briella rolled her eyes, "I cannot do any more damage, Force."

Always the gentleman, he kept his thoughts of that statement to himself. Unfortunately, the expression on his face told her precisely what was on his mind, and once again, the 'twins' had hurt her feelings.

Briella flew out of the window to sit on the bonnet of April's car. Scout swiftly followed to try to cheer up her friend. "Want to see if the kittens will let us ride them, Briella?"

"I know what you are doing, Scout. While I appreciate your efforts immensely, I am not in the mood." Briella hugged her knees to her chest.

"That's the point," Scout said, gently touching Briella's shoulder.

They sat in silence for a few minutes when there was a massive commotion by the industrial bins around the back. Scout and Briella flew over to investigate. Force was throwing the lid back on the one to the left, and Callum was hanging over the edge of the other by his waist.

"Oooh," Briella squealed. "What are they doing in the garbage bins?"

"I don't know," Scout replied, wrinkling her nose in disgust. "Why don't we ask them?"

"What are you looking for?" Briella shouted forcefully.

"The skeleton," Force hurriedly replied before Callum could share a sardonic comment.

Scout frowned, "Is he missing again?"

"Damn straight!" Callum snarled. "Made short work of getting out of those handcuffs."

"Really?" Briella marvelled, beginning to feel much better. *"Best of luck finding him."*

Force lifted his head and asked with an incredulous tone, "You are not going to help us look?"

Briella shook her head, *"We are not the ones who lost him. Find him yourselves."* Her tone was considerably brighter. Scout noticed the glint in her eye and worried that Briella had done something to help Skelly escape. She soon realised that the excitement exuding from Briella was for an entirely different reason. "Let's go," she encouraged, leading the way to their room.

They flew inside the window, and Briella went straight to the crate housing the bedding for the kittens. She approached Stubs and tugged his whiskers mildly. He swiped at her with a gentle paw, then went back to purring. Briella buzzed his ear and then shouted, "Wake up, Stubs!"

He jerked violently and then got to his feet, shaking his head fiercely. "What do you think you are doing waking me up like that?" he meowed.

Briella patted his nose in the spot he liked best. He closed his eyes with pleasure and purred more loudly. "I missed you, Stubs. Do you want to play?"

He peered at her with disbelieving eyes. "I was asleep. My siblings are asleep."

"Wake them up," Briella encouraged.

Scout laid a hand on Briella's arm. "What are you doing, Briella? They are babies. They need their sleep."

"Don't be silly, Scout. The kittens at home are always awake at this hour hunting for their food."

"They mustn't have humans who feed them," Scout countered. "Otherwise, they would be asleep like these guys."

"What's going on?" Snow asked, rubbing a paw over her eyes.

Briella puffed out her chest in triumph, "We are going to play a game."

Snow's eyes opened wider. "Oh, goodie. What is it called?"

"Jousting," Briella replied.

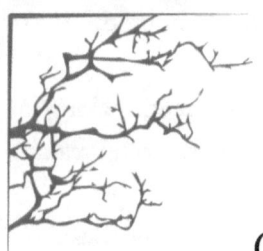

Chapter Nineteen

In the excitement of the moment, Briella began to leak fairy dust. Scout's breath hitched in her throat, and she let out a long, slow breath. The last thing she wanted was to spoil Briella's fun. Goodness knows she needed some in her life, now more than ever. The threat of having six fully grown cats in the confines of this small room until dawn, however, was enough to make Scout feel the need to say something.

"Are you sure this is a good idea, Briella?"

"Yeah," she replied, zooming past Scout on her way to the bathroom. Scout followed, nervously flapping her wings as Briella opened the door of the upper cabinet and attempted to lift the lid of a container holding cotton buds. A few more specks of fairy dust fluttered to the bottom of the basin, glistening attractively against the white of the porcelain.

"Your dust?" Scout mentioned cautiously.

"What about it?" Briella puffed, having another go at the lid.

"You are leaking."

Briella took her hands off the container and fluttered backward. "Oh," she uttered forlornly. "You are right. We shouldn't be doing this until after Halloween."

Scout viewed the slowing of Briella's wings, the dipping of her head, and the droop of her shoulders with a broken heart. Poor Briella. This was the happiest she had been since they started hunting Sarina, the Vampire Queen, and Scout had gone and taken that away from her. Damn it all! Dawn wasn't that far away that they couldn't manage the consequences of a bit of fun. Scout lifted her head defiantly, "Tell me what you need, and I will organise it. You will have your joust, Briella."

"Really!" Briella squealed with enthusiasm.

"We will need the jousting sticks I have hidden inside a drawer in my wardrobe, although we will need more if they get broken, and a divider of some sort to separate my area of the path from yours. The helmets from the garage will protect our heads, and we will wrap a couple of pillows around our chests for extra safety."

"How do you play this game exactly?"

"I sit on my kitten, and you sit on your kitten. Then we line up on opposite ends of the path and ride toward each other on opposite sides of the divider and try to knock each other off our kittens with the cotton tips. The first one to fall off their kitten loses. We will play best out of three, I think."

"You want to knock me off my kitten with a stick?"

"Yeah. The stick won't hurt when it hits you. It's got cotton on the top and bottom so it will be nice and soft.

Besides, you will be wearing a helmet and pillow for safety. It'll be loads of fun."

Scout didn't appear convinced. "How many times have you played this game?"

"None," Briella admitted. "But I have seen 'A Knight's Tale' many times, and it looks like heaps of fun. The people in the movie laugh and cheer for the person they want to win. I think some of them have more fun than the two people who are actually playing the game."

"I can't imagine why that would be," Scout's sarcasm was lost on Briella.

"They are so busy trying to win that they don't have the opportunity to get caught up in the atmosphere like the crowd does," she explained.

"Right," Scout said, realising Briella missed her point entirely. Rather than pull the pin, Scout decided she would try the game before she decided whether it was going to be as stupid as she believed it to be. Who knew, she might enjoy herself, though she highly doubted it. "Is there anything else we need to set up the game?"

"Yeah. I need a ruler from the bottom drawer in the kitchen and some of the packing foam that is lying beside the table where our new house is."

"Okay. I know that I promised not to use my magic until after Halloween. However, I may have to in order to acquire some of these items."

Briella's grin was infectious, "Go for it."

Scout used her dust to float the cotton tip container into the living area from Briella's wardrobe. She retrieved the ruler and packing foam, adding them to the pile of goodies. Then the fairies flew to their new house to retrieve the helmets that were inside their new garage. Once they were added to the pile on the floor, Briella gathered up the pillows from her bed and asked Scout for some sticky tape, also located in the bottom drawer in the kitchen.

Scout placed the small blocks of foam on the floor in a straight line. She grabbed the ruler, put it on top of the foam, and sawed it back and forward until the ruler stood on its own. Then, she flipped the lid on the cotton tips and drew out one for each of them. By this point, the kittens had come over and were trying to get their paws into the container to play with the cotton tips themselves. Scout and Briella were slapping their paws, but the kittens were bigger and were able to swat the fairies far better. Scout had the final laugh, however, closing the lid and watching the kittens trying to work out how to get to the goodies inside. Briella helped Scout secure her helmet and pillow, and then Scout did the same for Briella. They were about to mount their respective kittens when the sports bag suddenly moved.

"Ah," they gasped in unison.

"We are not going to panic," Scout muttered to herself.

"SCOUT!"

"It's okay, Briella." Scout took a steadying breath and fluttered above the bag. She peered inside and laughed so hard she nearly wet herself.

"What are you laughing at?" Briella queried, losing some of the fear that held her frozen to the spot.

"Come and see," Scout encouraged.

"I'd rather you just tell me." Briella suddenly had a thought, "Is one of the kittens stuck in there?"

"No," Scout answered, desperately trying to calm herself. "The skeleton is hiding in there."

Briella raced over to have a look. "You're kidding?" she said, peering inside. Her laughter was music to Scout's ears. She waited with bated breath to see if Briella would start leaking again. When she didn't, Scout threw her a question. "Do you think we should contact the boys and tell them?"

"No way," Briella answered, thinking of the fun the men would suck out of the evening. "Leave him be. He seems to be happy hiding in there."

"It must be squishy in there."

"He wouldn't stay if he didn't want to, Scout. The skeleton put himself in there."

"You are right. Let's have some fun." Scout raised the cotton tip and waved it about.

Briella raced toward her kitten and got herself comfortable. Then she brought her to the starting position and waited for Scout to take her place at the other end. "Best of three?"

"Best of three," Briella confirmed. "Ready! Set! Go!"

The kittens just stood there. Scout pressed her knees into Stub's shoulders. Briella kicked her feet against Snow's belly. The kittens still stood there.

"Perhaps we should explain the game to the kittens."

"You are absolutely correct," Briella responded, then proceeded to explain the rules to the kittens. As soon as she had finished speaking, the kittens ran toward each other. The fairies raised their jousts, and BOOM, they collided, both of them flailing aboard their mounts. Laughter filled the room as the kittens prepared to attack once more. Scout was the first to fall. Briella soon after. On and on, they went until the kittens tired and lay down on the floor. Scout and Briella high-fived one another. Scout giggled, "We will definitely have to play this again. I didn't think it would be as much fun as it was."

"Right!" Briella responded.

They were preparing to pack up when two very dejected men stepped into the room. Force sat on the couch and put his feet on the coffee table. "I don't know how we are going to find it in the daytime. We should have spotted him from kilometres away without any camouflage to hide his glow."

Callum agreed, choosing to sit at the dining table. "I guess your present is gone for good."

The fairies chuckled conspiratorially. "We found your skeleton."

"Where is it?" Callum leaned forward.

"In the bag he came in," Scout informed him.

Callum jumped off his chair and spread apart the material. "My goodness, he *is* in there."

"What a sneaky skeleton," Briella said.

Titles by Marnie Atwell

Battle Star Universe

Starlight Investigations

Jealousy Monsters

Vampire

Phantasm

Halloween Madness

The Pumpkin Patch

The House of Horrors

The Spirited Scarecrow

The Curious Kitten

The Sneaky Skeleton

About the Author

Marnie is an Australian author who lives in South-East Queensland with her husband and two children. When she is not dreaming up new adventures for her characters; Marnie enjoys creating digital art with Daz Studio, reading paranormal romance novels, and spending time with her family and friends. Not necessarily in that order.

Visit her website at: www.marnieatwell.com for more books, pictures, and downloads.

The final book in the Halloween Madness series is:

Halloween Hollow